Tasha The Last Princess Warrior

Tasha The Last Princess Warrior, Volume 1

Isaiah Fransen

Published by Isaiah Fransen, 2023.

TASHA THE LAST PRINCESS WARRIOR

First edition. February 14, 2023.

Copyright © 2023 Isaiah Fransen.

ISBN: 979-8215910092

Written by Isaiah Fransen.

Table of Contents

Dedication "Book Cover Design by ebooklaunch.com"

Chapter 1
Interesting Things Unfold

ONE DAY THERE WAS A princess named Tasha. Life was pretty boring for this young girl as she was always looking for adventure! However, she had no time for that kind of stuff, as she was very busy fulfilling her duties as princess. Meanwhile her dad, King Mike, and her mom Queen Sophie, were busy negotiating with their neighbors, and keeping the peace. One day, her dad, King Mike came upstairs and said, "our neighbors are coming to visit and we need you downstairs." She said, "OK, be right down!" Their neighbors were King Russell and Queen Petunia. They were always very grumpy and very rude to her dad King Mike and her mom,Queen Sophie, so Tasha headed downstairs. There she saw her dad King Mike, and her mom, Queen Sophie, both on their thrones. Just then, King Russell, and Queen Petunia arrived. They began talking about how to keep the peace between the two of them. King Russell and

Queen Petunia were asking about a certain sword that was supposedly hidden somewhere in the castle. However, King Mike and Queen Sophie said "it is top secret, and nobody can see the sword but them." King Russell and Queen Petunia said "well if we don't get to see the sword then you will pay" and they left the room. From the back of the room Tasha said "what was that all about?" King Mike replied "don't worry about it" "What is this sword you're speaking of?" asked Tasha. "It is a sword that used to belong to your sister," said King Mike.

"I had a sister?" replied Tasha. And King Mike said "yes, she was one of the few princess warriors who had a really powerful sword that had magical powers. Unfortunately she perished while battling in a war. Ever since then her sword has remained in the castle untouched. " King Mike said, "Anyways, we have to get ready for the royal fair which is happening later today." So Tasha said "ok, I will head back up to my room and get ready." Finally everyone was ready to leave the castle and go to the fair. They headed off into town to the fair. Once they arrived they were greeted by the villagers and everyone was having fun. There was a pie eating contest, a parade, and archery all taking place at the same time. And then all of a sudden they heard explosions at the castle and everyone in the village was panicking. King Mike, Queen Sophie, and Tasha all said " we need to get back to the castle right away".

Chapter 2
Castle Under Siege

KING MIKE, QUEEN SOPHIE, and Tasha were hurrying back to the castle as the castle was under attack! All of a sudden, when they got there they saw two guards that weren't theirs and they started to come after them! King Mike said, "Who are you and what do you want?" The guards quickly used their swords against them! King Mike tried to fight back, however, he was hit by one of their swords and was badly hurt! Queen Sophie and Tasha were like, "oh no!" They both took out the guards and headed over to King Mike. He was so badly hurt that he was dying! King Mike said, "you both must get to the sword before they do!" Tasha said "no dad, I can't leave you here!" Queen Sophie said, "we have no other choice I'm afraid dear!" Tasha was crying, but they both had to get to the sword!

They quickly left King Mike and headed inside the castle. Meanwhile, King Russell and Queen Petunia found the chamber where the sword was hidden. Shortly after however, Queen Sophie and Tasha stepped into the chamber and found them there! Queen Sophie said, "how could you guys do this, you don't know what power that sword holds!" "Oh yes we do, and it's going to make us the most powerful rulers of all the land!" Queen Sophie was like, "You have to be joking!" King Russell and Queen Petunia both said, "No we're not!" They sent more of their guards after Queen Sophie and Tasha! All of a sudden, King Russell grabbed the sword! However, the sword was too powerful and the chamber started to collapse! King Russell said to Queen Petunia, "forget the sword for now, we have to get out of here!" So they quickly escaped through another entrance to the chamber! However, before they left, they said, "that's it, we are going to war!" And as they left, Tasha was running for the exit and just made it! However, Queen Sophie was still at the other side of the chamber,and the chamber was starting to cave in! Queen Sophie yelled at Tasha, "you must take the sword!" So Queen Sophie threw the sword to Tasha and said,"only a princess can use the sword, goodbye Tasha!" Then the chamber collapsed, and queen Sophie was gone! Tasha was crying and said, "why did this have to happen?" Then she heard explosions coming from outside! She looked outside and saw the whole village was on fire! Tasha said, "I have to do something!"

Chapter 3
The War Begins

TASHA WAS ON HER WAY to the village as the village was on fire! She got there and found out that everyone was panicking! There were a bunch of guards trying to get everyone! She quickly pulled out the sword and said, "please sword, don't fail me now!" However when she used the sword to attack the guards, she felt something really different inside her! Suddenly, the sword caught fire and she was surprised! So she started to use the flaming sword against the guards, and the guards screamed "run!" And they all ran away! Then, all of a sudden, the sword turned to water and she used the water sword to put out the fires! Everyone was cheering for Tasha! Meanwhile, the guards headed back to King Russell and Queen Petunia's Castle and said to them, "we were attacked by the princess and the sword which turned to fire!" King Russell was like, "I want all guards to their battle stations, and I want the princess dead! I want the sword at all costs, even if you have to destroy villages to get it!" The guards were like, "yes sir!" They quickly got an army together and started heading out to get the princess and her sword! Meanwhile Tasha was on a walk through the woods when she spotted something unusual. It looked like a horse was trying to reach an apple off a tree but couldn't reach it. So Tasha used the sword to cut down the branch of apples off the tree, and gave an apple to the horse. She said, "here you go" and then she left. However, the horse started to follow her. She said, "Do you want to come along little guy?" So they headed back to the Village. When they got back however, the village was all gone, and the castle was completely destroyed! An army of guards were holding the villagers captive! Then they saw Tasha and the horse and said, "get her!" Tasha was like, "what am I going to do?" The horse was trying to get Tasha to hop on its back,and so she did! They quickly took off back into the forest!

Chapter 4
Deep Into The Forest

TASHA AND THE HORSE were trying to escape the army of guards that were chasing them! They came up to a cliff and they were surrounded by the army of guards! Tasha pulled out the sword,and all of a sudden it turned to ice! She used the sword to freeze the army of guards! They were frozen solid! Tasha said to the horse, That was a close one! What should I name you? I think I'll name you Max." The horse liked that name! All of a sudden they heard something! There was a troll coming out of the bushes, and suddenly there were a bunch of them! They all had bows and arrows! Then the leader of the trolls came out and said, "who disturbs our forest?" Tasha said "my name is Tasha, I'm a princess and this is my horse Max." The leader of the trolls said, "take them away back to our camp deep in the forest!" Tasha yelled, "no wait!" But it was too late, and the trolls tied Tasha and Max up, and took them away! When they got to the camp, the leader of the trolls said, "throw them into the fire!" Tasha yelled, "wait no!" and she pulled out her sword! The leader of the trolls said, "where did you get that?" Tasha said, "it was my sister's sword which was handed down to me after my mom and dad were killed recently!" The leader of the trolls said, "you wouldn't know who did that, would you?" Tasha said, "King Russell and Queen Petunia." The leader of the trolls said, "follow me!" Meanwhile one of the guards headed back to King Russell and Queen Petunia's castle and said to King Russell and Queen Petunia "our men were frozen by the sword and the Princess and her new horse were taken by trolls!" King Russell yelled "that's it, bring me the bounty hunter!" The guard said, "yes sir!" King Russell said "once the sword is mine, I will finish off the princess like I did with her sister all those years ago! No one will be able to stop us!" Meanwhile the leader of the trolls and Tasha sat down together and the leader of the trolls said, "I knew your sister, and that sword has great power. I see your heart is pure, so the sword will protect you. However, if it falls into the hands of someone whose heart is not pure, it will open up a portal and a creature of pure destruction will come out of the portal and destroy us all! You must make sure that it does not fall into King Russell's or Queen Petunia's hands! Also King Russell was the one that took your sister's life. You see, a long time ago there was another war for the sword. Back then, King Russell was a royal guard and he confronted your sister, and said, give me the sword! Your sister was completely surrounded, so she ended up giving up the sword but told the sword to disappear back to the castle where it came from, which was your castle. So the sword disappeared right out of her hands, and King Russell was so furious that he ended up taking your sister's life!" Tasha said, "that's terrible!"

Meanwhile back at King Russell and Queen Petunia's castle, the bounty hunter arrived and said, "my name is Pablo the bounty hunter, how can I be of service?" King Russell said "I need you to find the princess and her horse and the sword! Keep the princess and her horse alive and bring them back here, as I want to deal with them personally!" Pablo The Bounty Hunter Said, "don't worry, I won't let you down!"

Chapter 5

Face To Face With Pablo The Bounty Hunter

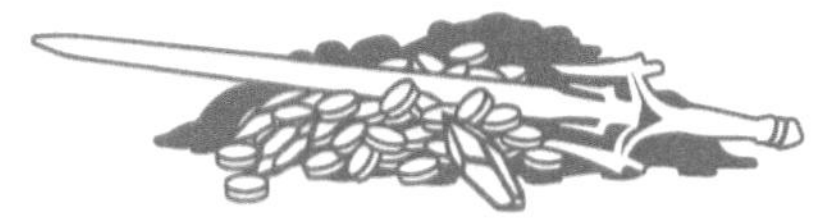

AS TASHA AND THE TROLLS were gathered around the fire discussing what plan of action they should take next, Pablo and his guards were quietly surrounding the camp.

Tasha's horse Max, sensing danger, started to get agitated. Tasha turning to Max asked, "what's wrong Max?" Seconds later a loud war call filled the air, and as Tasha spun around, there was the bounty hunter and all his guards charging towards them! Quickly,Tasha lifted her sword upwards and told it to freeze the army of guards that were quickly descending on them! Walking towards the one guard she had noticed wearing the symbol which revealed he was the leader, she touched his mouth with the tip of the sword. That melted the ice around his lips allowing him to speak. Tasha then spoke saying, "I demand you to reveal who you are and what is the reason for this attack?" The guard responded, "my name is Pablo and I'm a bounty hunter. I've been sent by King Russell and Queen Petunia to retrieve the sword as well as you and your horse. In return they have promised to pay a large amount of valuable coins." Tasha said "you won't get away with this". All of a sudden Pablo the bounty hunter broke free from the ice. Tasha and her horse started to run away! However, the trolls were captured by Pablo the bounty hunter and his guards and taken back to King Russell and Queen Petunia's castle. Pablo the bounty hunter said "I haven't been able to capture the princess and her sword and the horse however, I managed to capture the trolls". King Russell said "Do you take me for a fool, throw them in the dungeon and get me the sword, the princess and her horse"! Pablo the bounty hunter said "okay but you will have to pay me more if you want me to go back and get her, the sword, and the horse". King Russell yelled "are you kidding me, get me her and the sword and her horse now, otherwise I will throw you in the dungeon!" Pablo the bounty hunter said "Yes, sir" with a grudge.

Chapter 6
Going After The Princess

PABLO THE BOUNTY HUNTER headed back on his search for the princess, her sword, and the horse. He approached a village where there were tons of people and started asking around if anyone had seen the princess and her horse. Many people had not seen her and this infuriated Pablo. Pablo the Bounty Hunter told the people, "if you see her let me know, otherwise I will burn your village down to the ground before your eyes!" Meanwhile, the princess was heading out of the forest on her horse and saw a village in the distance. She got closer to the village to find out that Pablo the Bounty Hunter had just left. All of a sudden the people of the village turned on the Princess and her horse and began to chase them down. Tasha pulled out the sword and turned the villagers to ice so she could get away. Pablo the Bounty Hunter returned and saw the villagers frozen. Now, knowing that the princess was there, he quickly started searching the area and found nothing. This made Pablo even more angry and he was determined to catch the princess and her horse,so he left the village to go find her. Meanwhile, Tasha and her horse went down to the river and saw a raft. They both got onto the raft and started to head down stream. All of a sudden there was a great waterfall! Tasha and her horse had to try and get off the raft fast, so they both quickly jumped off the raft onto shore. It was getting dark out so they started to try to find a place to stay the night. Suddenly, to her surprise, she saw an old castle. They both went into the castle and went up the stairs to an old bedroom. They both went to sleep. All of a sudden they heard something like a growl, so they started to check everywhere! She looked out the window and saw a huge dragon!

Chapter 7
Return Of The Dragon

TASHA COULD NOT BELIEVE her eyes that there was a dragon out the window and it suddenly started to breathe fire! Tasha and her horse started to run down the staircase as the dragon was breathing fire through the windows of the castle! Tasha and her horse got outside and the dragon was right there! Tasha pulled out her sword and started to use the fire from her sword to fight the dragon. However, the fire was no match for the dragon! Tasha then decided to use the water from her sword to fight the dragon and that did not work either. Finally, Tasha used the ice and froze the dragon solid. Then Tasha and her horse made their escape! However the dragon broke free and started to chase Tasha and her horse! Eventually, Tasha and her horse ended up at a dead end and had nowhere to go! Tasha had no choice but to fight for her life! She quickly turned the sword to fire again and started to fight the dragon. Tasha tried to keep the dragon away from them while they could find a way to escape. Eventually they managed to get past the dragon and they kept running away from the dragon! Eventually they came to a cliff and Tasha had an idea. She tried to fight the dragon and quickly used her sword on fire and tried to get the dragon to fall off the cliff. The dragon used his fire breath against Tasha, but Tasha used the water from her sword to extinguish the flame! Finally, the dragon lost his grip and fell off the edge of the cliff! Tasha checked to see if the dragon was still alive. She could not see the dragon and she said, "the dragon is probably not alive anymore!" She then got back on her horse and took off again.

Chapter 8
Tasha Vs Pablo The Bounty Hunter

WHILE TASHA WAS BUSY dealing with the dragon, Pablo the bounty hunter had made his way to the river. He searched and searched until he stumbled upon the raft. Now he knew the Princess, her horse, and the sword had to be close. He headed to where he saw the old castle and saw that a conflict had just recently happened there. Meanwhile, Tasha was heading back to the old castle when she spotted Pablo The Bounty Hunter outside. Tasha quickly jumped on her horse and they started to run away as fast as they could. Pablo The Bounty Hunter started chasing them and eventually they both came up to the river. There was nowhere left to run. Pablo The Bounty Hunter said, "this is the end of the line for you and your horse and the sword!" Tasha said "no it is not, I will fight till my last breath!" She pulled out the sword and started to take on Pablo The Bounty Hunter! Pablo quickly reached for his sword but Tasha's sword was too powerful for him! All of a sudden the dragon returned and they were both shocked. However, the bounty hunter knew how to get the dragon to obey him. He used his hands to direct the dragon in ways that he wanted. Then Tasha and her horse realized they were both in trouble. So Pablo The Bounty Hunter actually managed to hop on the dragon's back. Tasha said to her horse, "we need to get out of here fast!" Pablo The Bounty Hunter was flying through the air on the dragon trying to catch Tasha and her horse and the sword. The dragon started to breathe fire and lit the forest on fire and Tasha and her horse were running for their lives.

Chapter 9

Escaping The Dragon And Pablo The Bounty Hunter

TASHA AND HER HORSE Max were running for their lives from Pablo the bounty hunter and his dragon! Tasha said to her horse, "We have to find a way out of here or he will burn the forest down with us in it". Tasha thought to herself, "there must be a way to distract Pablo the bounty hunter so we can get away". Tasha came up with the brilliant idea to distract Pablo and his dragon by using a fake sword to give to him. Tasha pulled out an old sword from her saddle bag and disguised the sword as the sword that Pablo wanted. Tasha left the fake sword in the middle of the forest and hid behind a nearby tree, patiently waiting for Pablo and his dragon. Pablo and his dragon were scouring around the forest and stumbled upon the sword that Tasha left. Pablo picked up the sword and said "Finally! I have the sword"! Pablo headed back to King Russell and Queen Petunia's castle to give them the sword. Meanwhile, Tasha couldn't believe that he actually fell for it. Tasha and her horse could escape! However, Tasha knew that she needed to separate Pablo the bounty hunter and his dragon. Meanwhile, Pablo the bounty hunter and his dragon arrived back at King Russell's and Queen Petunia's castle. Pablo presented King Russell with the sword. King Russell took the sword from Pablo and said "Wait! This is not the sword, this is a fake"! Pablo the bounty hunter said "I am so sorry King Russell". King Russell was furious and said "I have had enough of you, guards throw Pablo in the dungeon". However, just in time the dragon appeared to save Pablo from the king and together they flew off.

Chapter 10
The Great Troll Escape

THE LEADER OF THE TROLLS and all of his trolls were stuck in King Russell and Queen Petunia's dungeon. The leader of the trolls said to the other trolls, "we have to find a way out of here!" There was a guard patrolling the dungeon to make sure all of the prisoners were accounted for. The leader of the trolls had an idea to escape by tricking the guard to think that there was one troll missing. So, the leader of the trolls decided to hide and the guard came past and saw that one of the trolls was missing. The guard opened up the cell and all of a sudden all of the trolls attacked him. The leader of the trolls quickly said "let's make a run for it!" They started to run up the stairs to get back to their forest. But suddenly, there were a bunch of guards waiting for them! The leader of the trolls said, "headback the other way!" The trolls headed back towards the dungeon to find a different escape route but were confronted by the previous guard. The guard caught the trolls and put them back in their cell. However, the leader of the trolls had another idea. Before the guard closed the cell up the leader of the trolls said "oh no, there's a dragon outside of the castle!" The guard looked outside to see the dragon and realized that there was nothing there and before he knew it,the trolls escaped and he was locked in the cell! The leader of the trolls said, "we have to find another way out of the dungeon!" They devised a plan to divide the trolls into two groups. The first group went up the same stairs to distract guards, while the second group found a way to attack the guards from behind. So, the first group of trolls went up the stairs and there were the guards waiting for them! This time the trolls had a plan. All of a sudden, the second group of trolls snuck up behind the guards and attacked them, allowing the trolls to finally escape the dungeon. The trolls all headed back to the forest.

Chapter 11
The Last Straw

KING RUSSELL HEARD that the trolls had escaped and said, "this is the last straw!" Queen Petunia said to King Russell, "what are we going to do?" King Russell said, "we are both going after the princess ourselves, get our horse carriage ready, and we will go deal with the princess personally!" Shortly after, King Russell and Queen Petunia headed off to find the princess. Meanwhile, Tasha and Max were at another village trying to make a plan to get Pablo the bounty hunter and his dragon separated. However, Tasha heard something out in the distance, it was King Russell and Queen Petunia's carriage and their guards riding in from the distance. Tasha realized that she had to get away as fast as she could! However, it was too late! King Russell and Queen Petunia arrived and saw Tasha and her horse and ordered the guards to seize her! Tasha quickly pulled out her sword and started to fight the guards and took them all out.

However, King Russell came out of the carriage and pulled out his sword. Tasha and King Russell started to fight. Tasha was gaining the upper hand because of her sword. However, King Russell had something up his sleeve that Tasha wasn't prepared for. King Russell had more guards coming the other way to ambush Tasha and her horse. Tasha was surrounded and had nowhere to go. All of a sudden, out of nowhere, the trolls came and took on all of the guards! King Russell and Queen Petunia were taken captive by the trolls. The leader of the trolls said to King Russell and Queen Petunia, "this is the end of the line for the two of you!" However, then Pablo the bounty hunter on his dragon came down from the sky to rescue King Russell and Queen Petunia to gain their loyalty back. King Russell and Queen Petunia hopped on the dragon with Pablo the bounty hunter and took off leaving the guards to fend for themselves. Eventually the trolls and Tasha took out all of the guards. However, the leader of the trolls said, "we need to get King Russell and Queen Petunia and stop them from getting your sword and unleashing the creature of pure destruction!"

Chapter 12
Alliance

TASHA AND THE TROLLS headed back to the trolls' camp to discuss what to do about King Russell and Queen Petunia and Pablo the bounty hunter and his dragon. The leader of the trolls told Tasha that they should both team up to stop King Russell and Queen Petunia and Pablo the bounty hunter and his dragon from getting the sword. The leader of the trolls said "we must attack first before they find us and get the upper hand. We must start with Pablo the bounty hunter and his dragon as they pose a big threat to the sword and the villagers safety!" So, Tasha and the trolls devised a plan to capture Pablo the bounty hunter and his dragon. Meanwhile, King Russell and Queen Petunia and Pablo the bounty hunter were back at King Russell's and Queen Petunia's castle, hatching a scheme to find a way to get the sword from Tasha. Pablo the bounty hunter said, "I have a plan." So, Pablo the bounty hunter took off on his dragon. Meanwhile, Tasha and the trolls were heading towards King Russell and Queen Petunias castle. Pablo the bounty hunter and his dragon spotted them in the distance and headed down to the ground for a surprise attack. Just then, Pablo the bounty hunter noticed that Tasha and the troll were starting to run away! Pablo the bounty hunter was hot on their tail! Just then, Pablo the bounty hunter and his dragon came up to a dark cave and saw Tasha and the trolls go inside the cave. All of a sudden,Pablo the bounty hunter realized it was a trap and Tasha used the sword on fire to knock the rocks and trap Pablo the bounty hunter and the dragon inside! To her surprise, it worked! Tasha and the trolls were celebrating! The leader of the trolls said "now we have to get to King Russell and Queen Petunia's castle to stop them once for all!"

Chapter 13
Ambush

TASHA AND THE TROLLS were on their way to King Russells and Queen Petunia's castle. All of a sudden, King Russell and Queen Petunia and their guards ambushed Tasha and the trolls! King Russell and Queen Petunia said to the guards, "attack!" So, Tasha and the trolls were fighting to their last breath to take out the guards and protect the sword. However, Tasha and the trolls were eventually all captured and taken back to King Russell and Queen Petunias castle. King Russell said, "Put them in the dungeon, except for Princess Tasha, take Princess Tasha to the throne room!" King Russell and Queen Petunia met Tasha in the throne room to decide her fate and secure the sword. King Russell said to Princess Tasha, "give me the sword and Tasha said, "never!" So, the guards took the sword out of Tashas hands and gave it to King Russell. King Russell said, "Finally, I have the sword, and now I am going to end

Princess Tasha's life!" But before he could, the sword turned black! All of a sudden, a portal opened up in the sky, and a huge creature with black scales and horns appeared and came down from the sky and landed in King Russells and Queen Petunia's throne room. To their surprise, the creature could speak, and said, "I am free at last, and now this world will meet its end!" King Russell and Queen Petunia said "who are you!" Tasha said, "I tried to keep the sword away from you! Now look at what you have done and unleashed on the world!" And the creature of pure destruction said to Tasha, "I have been waiting for many moons to be unleashed!" King Russell and Queen Petunia's guards started to attack the creature, however, the creature ate all of the guards! All of a sudden, King Russell and Queen Petunia started to run, however, the creature of pure destruction ate King Russell and Queen Petunia. Tasha quickly picked up the sword and started to fight the creature with the sword on ice. Tasha managed to temporarily freeze the creature of pure destruction using the ice sword, using that as her chance to get away from the creature. Then, Tasha freed the trolls from the dungeon and ran back with the trolls to the trolls camp. The creature of pure destruction freed himself from the ice and said, "finally I can destroy this world and no one can stop me!"

Chapter 14

The Creature Of Pure Destruction's Reign

BACK AT THE CAMP TASHA and the trolls realized they had a whole new threat to deal with. King Russell, Queen Petunia and the majority of the guards were gone, but unfortunately not before they let loose the Creature of Pure Destruction! Now they had a whole new problem on their hands! "How are we going to destroy this horrible creature?" Tasha asked the trolls. The leader of the trolls said to Tasha, "the only way to destroy the creature is to use the sword and imprison it back into the sword! The only way you can imprison the creature back into it, is to fight the creature, and get him weak enough to imprison him back into the sword!" However, the last person who had originally imprisoned the creature was imprisoned into the sword along with the creature of pure destruction. Meanwhile, as they were in deep discussion about what to do, back at the castle, the creature of pure destruction was contriving a plan himself! He thought to himself that he would go and destroy the villages one by one until he reached his final destination, the troll's camp.

Chapter 15
Villages On Fire

THE CREATURE OF PURE destruction headed towards his first village and started to reign terror on the villagers, destroying the whole village with one fiery blow. Meanwhile, Tasha and her horse Max left the trolls' camp to find the creature of pure destruction.They came up to the village and they discovered that the village was in flames! The creature of pure destruction was nowhere in sight. It appeared that the creature of pure destruction had just left. Tasha was in shock, she could not believe her eyes and the catastrophic scene! Tasha put out the fire with her sword with water but saw that the villagers were badly hurt! Just then, the leader of the trolls came and saw all of the villagers that were badly hurt and said, "we should get them back to the trolls camp so we can heal them." So, the leader of the trolls got all of his trolls and started carrying the villagers to safety, one by one, taking the most seriously wounded first.

One of the villagers on the way out told Tasha that the creature of pure destruction was headed to the other villages. So Tasha said, "I must get to the other villages before the creature of pure destruction does!" Meanwhile, Pablo the bounty hunter and his dragon broke out of the cave and noticed everything that was going on. Pablo said, "hmm, this is the perfect opportunity for me to do a sneak attack on Tasha!"

Chapter 16
Return Of Pablo The Bounty Hunter

TASHA AND MAX WERE on their way to the next village. When they got there, they warned everyone to evacuate the village. But the creature of pure destruction arrived before everyone was able to evacuate! Tasha pulled out her sword and started to fight the creature of pure destruction so as to give the villagers time to escape. However, just as the creature of pure destruction was going to finishTasha off, Pablo the bounty hunter swooped down on his dragon. The creature of pure destruction said, "what is the meaning of this? Don't you know who I am, and what terror I am capable of?" Pablo the bounty hunter said, "Take this!" and then Pablo the bounty hunter's dragon blew fire at the creature of pure destruction" The creature of pure destruction had to retreat to avoid the flames. Pablo the bounty hunter headed towards Tasha and her horse! Tasha said to Pablo the bounty hunter, "what do you want, and how did you escape the cave?" Pablo the bounty hunter said, "I am here to finish you off Tasha, once and for all, come fight me!" Tasha said "I don't have time for you right now! The creature of pure destruction is on the loose, and if I don't stop him, he will destroy the entire world!" Pablo the bounty hunter said, "I don't care about your problems, come fight me!" Tasha quickly hopped on her horse and started to run away from Pablo the bounty hunter! Pablo the bounty hunter hopped on his dragon and started to chase them down! Eventually, Tasha and her horse came to a dead end and had no choice but to pull out her sword and fight Pablo the bounty hunter and his dragon head on!

Chapter 17

Tasha And Pablo The Bounty Hunter's Truce

TASHA AND PABLO THE bounty hunter were fighting each other when Tasha said to Pablo the bounty hunter, "there is no time for this! I need to stop the creature of pure destruction before he destroys the entire world!" Pablo the bounty hunter said, "you left my dragon and I in a cave to die, why should I let you stop this creature?" Tasha said, "if you don't stop fighting with me you will have nothing left to fight for!" Pablo thought about it and said "hmm.. maybe you're onto something! What's in it for me?" Tasha said, "your life!" Then, Pablo the bounty hunter came to his senses. So Pablo the bounty hunter said toTasha, "how about a truce until the creature is destroyed.?" So, Pablo the bounty hunter and Tasha came to an agreement. They both headed off to face the creature together. Tasha and Pablo the bounty hunter headed to the next village where the creature of pure destruction was reigning terror. Tasha quickly used her sword to distract the creature while Pablo the bounty hunter led the villagers to safety on his dragon. Tasha's sword all of a sudden changed color and started to turn to a gold color. The creature of pure destruction said, "no not again!" All of a sudden, Tasha's feet started to lift off the ground while holding the sword. The creature of pure destruction said, "I must stop the sword from trapping me into the sword again!" The creature tried to attack the sword at which point the sword broke in half to the surprise of Tasha. The creature of pure destruction was pleased and said, "now nothing can stop me!" Tasha was not happy and fell to her knees and started to cry, and said, "what am I going to do now without the sword?" So, Pablo the bounty hunter said to Tasha, "we have to get out of here." Pablo the bounty hunter and Tasha hopped on his dragon and started to fly towards the trolls camp to see what to do with the sword.

Chapter 18
Repairing The Sword

TASHA AND PABLO THE bounty hunter arrived at the trolls camp where they were both met by the leader of the trolls. The leader of the trolls said to Tasha, "Wait, what is he doing here?" Tasha said, "we made a truce because of the creature of pure destruction!" Pablo interrupted Tasha and the leader of the trolls, and said, "I don't want to be here just as much as you don't want me to be here, but the world is at stake!" Then Tasha showed the leader of the trolls the broken sword. The leader of the trolls said, "oh no!" The leader of the trolls said, "the only way to repair the sword is to find a special kind of metal only found in a cave inside a mountain, which is the most dangerous mountain in the entire kingdom! The mountain is unstable, and it is rumored there is a giant inside the cave!" Tasha said, "we have to get the metal somehow without the giant noticing." So Tasha headed off on her horse, while Pablo the bounty hunter headed off on his dragon to get the metal and repair the sword. Tasha and Pablo the bounty hunter arrived at the base of the mountain and started heading up the path towards the cave. However, Tasha and Pablo the bounty hunter made too much noise which caused a rock slide. Tasha yelled to Pablo, the bounty hunter, "we have to run for it!" Quickly, they both just made it into the cave just in time. Tasha and Pablo the bounty hunter found themselves trapped in the cave with Tasha's horse and Pablo the bounty hunter's dragon.

Chapter 19
Facing The Giant

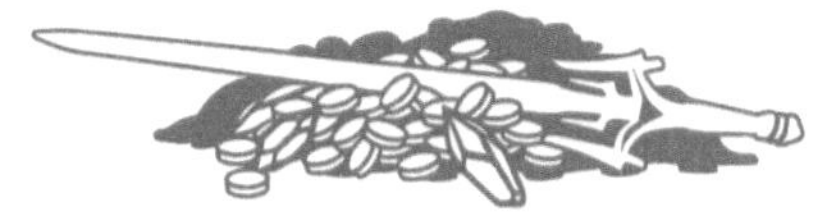

BOTH TASHA AND PABLO the bounty hunter were trapped in the cave and they decided to go deeper into the cave. They came up to a cavern which appeared to be occupied. Tasha saw a giant pot on top of a fire and it smelt like something was cooking in the pot. Pablo the bounty hunter said, "what is this?" Then all of a sudden a big hand came down and picked them both up! It was the giant and he said, "goodie, now I have my supper! I will put you both in a cage and cook the two of you for supper!" Tasha and Pablo the bounty hunter screamed, "please don't eat us! We were just here to get the special metal to fix our sword!" The giant said, "I don't care, you look too tasty for me to give you up!" The giant put them both in a cage and left them there while he prepared the pot. All of a sudden, the giant heard a strange sound! It was Pablo the bounty hunter's dragon! The dragon and Tasha's horse started to charge the giant! Meanwhile,

Pablo the bounty hunter and Tasha were trying to find a way to escape the cage. Pablo the bounty hunter had an idea, he pulled out something from his pocket. It was a knife, and he started to pick the lock of the cage. Eventually, the cage opened and they both escaped! However, they still had to get past the giant. Tasha quickly hopped onto her horse and Pablo the bounty hunter hopped onto his dragon and started to fight the giant. Eventually, they led the giant to the cave entrance which had been blocked, and moved out of the way just in time as the giant busted through the cave entrance. The giant ran too fast from the cave and fell off a cliff to his death!

Chapter 20
Finding The Metal

TASHA AND PABLO THE bounty hunter headed back into the cave to find the special metal to fix the sword. Tasha and Pablo the bounty hunter went deep into the cave until they came to another cavern and saw a metal protruding from a rock. Tasha grabbed another rock and started chipping away at the rock in the cavern to see what it was. Sure enough, it was the metal that they were searching for. So, Tasha and Pablo the bounty hunter headed out of the cave and back to the trolls camp with the special metal in hand. But when they got to the trolls camp the creature of pure destruction was there destroying it. The leader of the trolls said, "we must get the sword back together! Quick, give me the metal!" Tasha gave the leader of the trolls the special metal they found in the cave. The leader of the trolls started to craft the metal together and sure enough the sword was fixed. Now the question was, does it still have its magical powers?

Tasha said, "there is only one way to find out!" So, Tasha tried to use the sword, and sure enough it was working! She used the sword on fire to fight the creature of pure destruction. The creature of pure destruction said, "how is this possible? You fixed the sword?" The creature of pure destruction said, "I must now finish you off personally!" So, the creature of pure destruction tried to finish off Tasha! However, once they both tried to fight each other the sword started to glow a gold color again. Tasha's feet started to lift off of the ground and the creature of pure destruction's feet also started to lift off of the ground. All of a sudden, they both disappeared.

Chapter 21
Inside The Sword

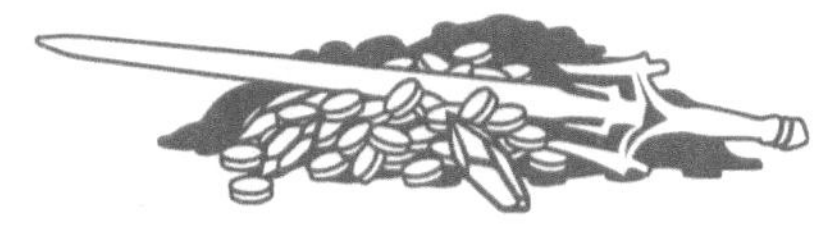

TASHA AND THE CREATURE pure destruction landed in an unknown realm! Tasha said, "where are we?" The creature of pure destruction said, "this is the realm of no return where I was imprisoned for 50 years! However, here I am your worst nightmare, as I am more powerful than ever here!" The creature of pure destruction then started to grow until he was gigantic! Then, before Tasha could run away, she suddenly came up to what appeared to be an old man! The old man said, "Come with me if you want to live!" Then the old man pulled out what appeared to be a magic wand and opened up a portal, and they both went in! The creature of pure destruction was like, "no! I will find you both!" Meanwhile, Tasha and the old man we're in a hidden cave in the new realm! Tasha asked, "Who are you?" The old man said, "I am a wizard named Travis." Tasha realized, "you must be the one that originally trapped the creature of pure destruction in the sword?" "You're right, I was," said Travis the wizard. Tasha asked, "is there any way to get out of here?" Travis the wizard said, "yes, however, the only way to get out of here is to destroy the creature of pure destruction! To do that, you must have the sword." "But I don't have the sword, it's back where we came from!" said Tasha. "Yes," said Travis the wizard, "however, there is a way to get the sword to come Into this realm! We must collect 3 crystals that are scattered throughout the realm in order to bring the sword here! I did try myself, however, the creature of pure destruction would not let me get them! However, with you here, maybe there is a way!" Tasha said, "I understand. What's the plan?"

Chapter 22
Collecting The 3 Crystals

TRAVIS THE WIZARD WENT up to the creature of pure destruction and the creature of pure destruction said, "If it isn't in my old friend Travis the wizard!" Travis the wizard said, "prepare to meet your end!" So Travis the wizard used his magic wand to fight the creature! Meanwhile, Tasha was looking for the first crystal. Suddenly she saw a light in the distance! She quickly went up to the light and found the first crystal! She grabbed it and put it in her pocket. Now she needed to find the second crystal. Then Tasha noticed something that appeared to be another cave! She saw another glowing light coming from the cave, so she went into the cave and there was the second crystal! She grabbed it and put it in her pocket. Tasha said, "now I only have one more crystal to find!" Then she noticed another glowing light far in the distance. It was coming from behind where Travis the wizard was fighting the creature pure destruction! Tasha said, "how am I going to get past them?" Meanwhile, Travis the wizard was still fighting the creature of pure destruction! Then the creature of pure destruction realized something! Tasha wasn't there with Travis the wizard! Then all of a sudden the creature of pure destruction realized the whole fight was a distraction! Then the creature of pure destruction spotted Tasha running towards the light behind him. The creature of pure destruction was like, "no, I must stop her now!" But it was too late, Tasha got the last crystal and then the crystals magically came together and brought the sword into the realm.

Chapter 23
Escaping The Realm

TASHA USED THE SWORD on fire against the creature of pure destruction! The creature of pure destruction was like, "no!" Then the creature of pure destruction started to breathe fire! Tasha turned the sword to water and put out the flames! Then Tasha turned the sword to ice and froze the creature temporarily! Tasha used the sword to open up a portal to get her and Travis the wizard back into the real world.Once they both got back to the real world the portal closed.The leader of the trolls, and all the trolls, and Pablo the bounty hunter were like, "hooray you did it!" However, Travis the wizard said, "no you didn't!" All of a sudden another portal opened up in the sky and the creature of pure destruction came back into the real world! However now the portal was sucking the real world up and Tasha was like, "what is going on!" Travis the wizard said, "do you remember how I told you that you had to destroy the creature of pure destruction before coming back to the real world? Well this is why! The creature of pure destruction now has the power of the sword and is using its powers to suck your world into the sword! Eventually your whole world will end up in the realm of no return where we just came from!" Tasha said, "we have to do something!" However, when Tasha tried to use the sword, it wasn't working! Travis the wizard said, "it's because the creature of pure destruction now has all the sword's power!" Tasha said "oh no! What are we going to do!"

Chapter 24

The Final Battle Between Tasha And The Creature Of Pure Destruction

EVERYONE'S FEET STARTED to lift off the ground and they were getting pulled into the portal! Travis the wizard shouted, "everyone hold on!" However, Tasha used the sword and stuck it into the ground! They were all holding on to each other while trying to avoid being sucked into the portal! The creature of pure destruction said, "you can try, but you can't hold on forever! Pretty soon this world will be destroyed, and I will be victorious!" However, just then, something was going on with the sword! Tasha noticed that the sword was turning white and ended up closing the portal! Everyone fell down to the ground but were safe! The creature of pure destruction was like, "no this can't be happening!" Then suddenly the sword had electricity going around it! Tasha pulled the sword from the ground and felt something that she had never felt before! All of a sudden clouds and lightning started to form around her and she started to float above the ground! Suddenly she was more powerful than the creature of pure destruction! The creature of pure destruction was like, "no this can't be! I must stop her now! I will be victorious! I cannot be defeated by a little princess!" Tasha said, "what did you just call me? I'm not a little princess! I am the Princess Warrior!" The creature used his fire breath trying to destroy Tasha! However, his attacks were blocked by the force field she put around the creature of pure destruction! He was defenseless! Suddenly, Tasha came down, at the speed of lightning, to attack the creature! Sure enough, the creature was destroyed! Everyone was cheering for Tasha! However, Pablo the bounty hunter wasn't, and said, "next time we meet we will be enemies!" Pablo the bounty hunter then hopped on his dragon and left! The leader of the trolls said, "we must get him!" Tasha said, "let him go, we will deal with him later!" Travis the wizard said "I don't know about you, but I think this calls for celebration!"

Chapter 25
The Celebration

EVERYONE WAS CELEBRATING after Tasha defeated the creature of pure destruction. All the trolls were dancing, Travis the wizard was cooking a stew for everyone, and Tasha was doing bow and arrow practice. Everyone was having such a good time! However, the leader of the trolls noticed Tasha didn't seem too happy. Later that night, the leader of the trolls invited Tasha into his tent and asked, "what seems to be bothering you Tasha?" Tasha said, "I miss my mom and dad. I don't know what to do now as I have defeated the creature of pure destruction! Now I don't know where to go from here." The leader of the trolls said, There are other adventures waiting for you! " You have just got to find them!" Tasha said, "where do I start?" The leader of the trolls said, "I do sense something else is coming, but I don't know what. Whatever it is, we must be prepared! I think the first thing to do is to find Pablo the bounty hunter to see what we're up against!" Tasha said, "I understand." Quickly Tasha hopped on her horse Max and started her journey to find Pablo the bounty hunter. The leader of the trolls and the trolls waved goodbye! The leader of the trolls said to himself, "stay safe PrincessTasha!" Meanwhile Pablo the bounty hunter was in a village nearby. All of a sudden he saw tasha! Tasha saw him, and Pablo the bounty hunter started to run away! Tasha hopped on her horse and yelled to her horse Max, "after him!" So they quickly went after him. Pablo the bounty hunter eventually came to a dead end in the village! Tasha said, "there is nowhere left to run Pablo!"Pablo the bounty hunter said, "if you want a fight you've got one!"

Chapter 26

Tasha And Pablo The Bounty Hunter's Rematch

TASHA PULLED OUT HER sword and was ready to fight Pablo the bounty hunter! Then Pablo the bounty hunter quickly reached for his sword and they both started to fight! However, somehow, Pablo the bounty hunter was gaining the upper hand! That didn't make sense, as Tasha's sword was magic! Pablo the bounty hunter explained, "you think you're the only one with a magic sword! Not anymore! I have a magic sword now too!" Tasha asked, "Where did you get that sword?" Pablo the bounty hunter said, "none of your concern!" He quickly used the sword on fire and started a fire in the village! Pablo the bounty hunter then hopped on his dragon and said, "see you around!" Tasha then quickly turned her sword to water and put out the fire in the village! Tasha said to herself, "what just happened?" Meanwhile Pablo the bounty hunter headed to this old castle where his new client was waiting. He said, "I got what you were asking for from the village mistress!" The client said, "good, now I can put an end to that imposter, and the Dark Princess Warrior will rule once again!"

The End

About the Author

Isaiah who has autism resides in the beautiful Okanagan Valley which is situated in the Southern part of British Columbia, Canada. Taking in the latest movies at the local theaters is one of his favorite pass times. His interest in solving mysteries has lead to his desire to write about them. His books is full of exciting plots and adventures. Playing video games keeps him busy the majority of his time but finds time in his sometimes hectic schedule to write and looks forward to publishing more of his work.